WHERE'S WALDO?
DOUBLE TROUBLE
AT THE MUSEUM

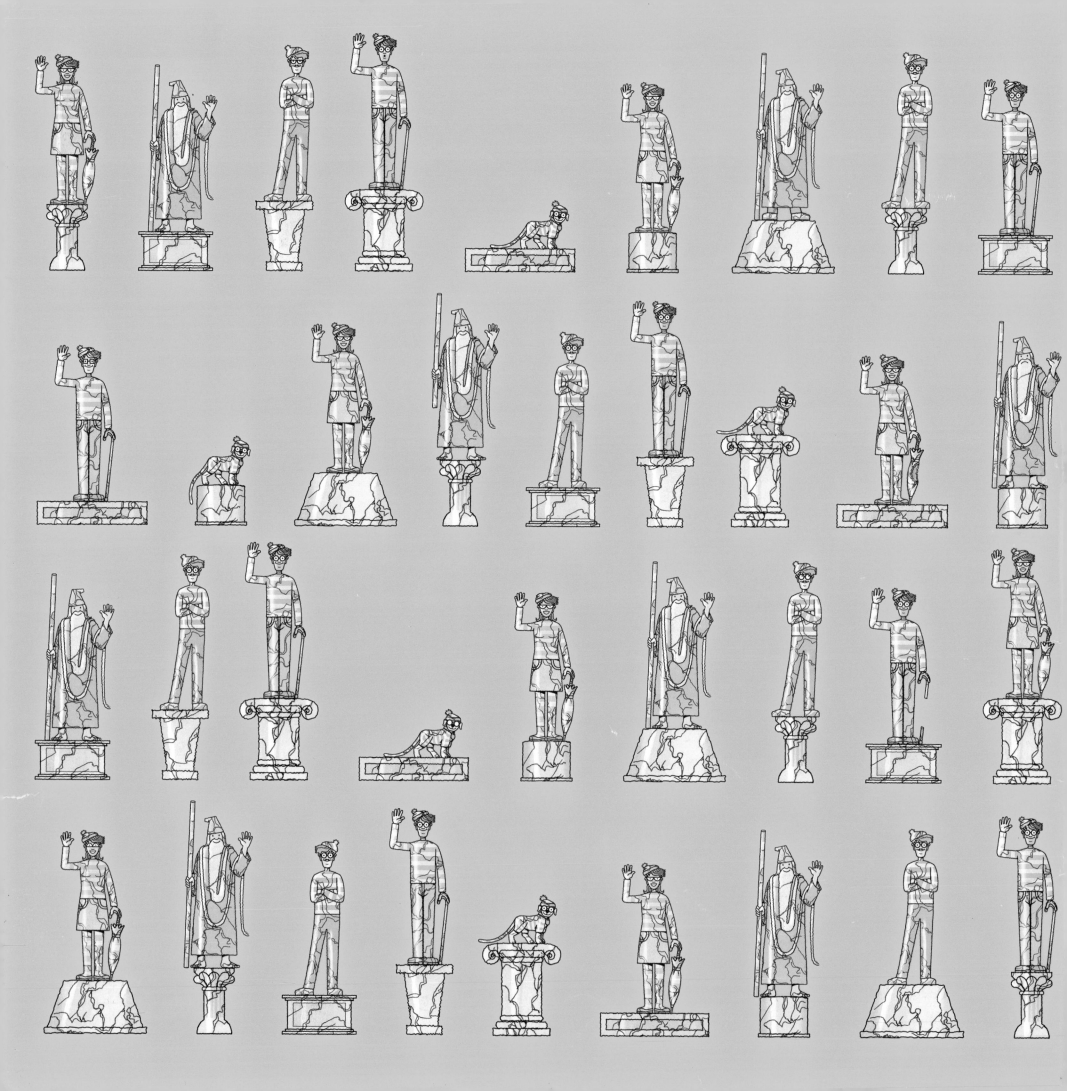

THE HALL OF STATUES

Wow! Look at these splendid statues! Each one has a match . . . except one thing has changed! Can you find the pairs, and then spot the differences?

First US paperback edition 2022

Library of Congress Catalog Card
Number 2019940108
ISBN 978-1-5362-0139-0
(hardcover)
ISBN 978-1-5362-2440-5
(paperback)

22 23 24 25 26 27 WKT
10 9 8 7 6 5 4 3

Printed in Shenzhen, Guangdong, China

This book was typeset in
Optima and Wallyfont.

The illustrations were done in ink
and watercolor or in ink and colored
digitally.

Candlewick Press
99 Dover Street
Somerville, Massachusetts 02144

visit us at www.candlewick.com

CANDLEWICK PRESS

WHERE'S WALDO?

DOUBLE TROUBLE

AT THE MUSEUM

MARTIN HANDFORD

HI THERE, WALDO FANS! I'M OFF FOR A DAY AT THE MUSEUM. AND THIS TIME, THERE'S DOUBLE THE FUN!

EACH SCENE IS FULL OF DEVILISHLY DIFFICULT DIFFERENCES. CAN YOU SPOT ALL THE CHANGES AMONG THE AMAZING ARTIFACTS AND EXCITING EXHIBITIONS?

DON'T FORGET TO LOOK FOR ME ON EVERY PAGE! AND THERE'S WOOF (BUT USUALLY ALL YOU CAN SEE IS HIS TAIL), WENDA, WIZARD WHITEBEARD, AND ODLAW. THEN FIND OUR FIVE LOST THINGS: MY KEY, WENDA'S CAMERA, WOOF'S BONE, WIZARD WHITEBEARD'S SCROLL, AND ODLAW'S BINOCULARS. THAT'S NOT ALL! MY FRIENDS AND I — AND OUR LOST THINGS — HAVE MOVED TO A NEW PLACE BETWEEN EACH PAIR OF SCENES. THAT'S TEN EXTRA DIFFERENCES TO SPOT ON EVERY PAGE!

WHAT MADNESS! WE'D BETTER GET GOING!

Waldo

Other than me and my friends, each character appears in the line twice.

But something has changed!

Can you spot all the differences?

WAY IN

EVEN IN THE ENTRANCE HALL, THERE IS MAYHEM IN THE MUSEUM! CAN YOU SPOT ALL THE DIFFERENCES?

THE ENTRANCE HALL

Spot five differences among the security guards.

Spot five differences among the displays.

Spot five differences among the visitors.

15 DIFFERENCES

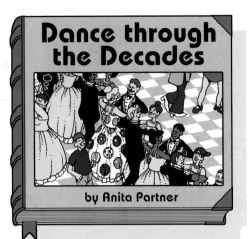

Dance through the Decades

by Anita Partner

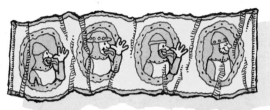

Musical Methods

by Dewey Sing

CHAPTER 2: DIVINATION

Some fortune-tellers predicted that the future was coming.

A Guide to Brushwork

by Horace Shu

Ivanna Scare **HAUNTED HAPPENINGS**

Sir Cumference **KNIGHTS TO REMEMBER**

Musical Methods

by Dewey Sing

A History of Horticulture

by Dan DeLion

TREASURES TO TREASURE

BY EMMA RULD

Many dinosaurs roamed the earth.

One herbivorous dinosaur was the Triceratops.

LEARNING THE ROPES

BY HARVEY WEIGHT

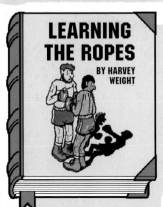

THE READING ROOM

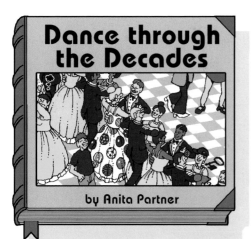

Dance through the Decades

by Anita Partner

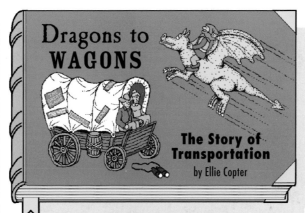

Dragons to WAGONS

The Story of Transportation

by Ellie Copter

A Guide to Brushwork by Horace Shu

A SHORT HISTORY OF TIME

T. K. Tock

TREASURES TO TREASURE

BY EMMA RULD

Many dinosaurs roamed the earth.

One herbivorous dinosaur was the Tricerabottoms.

Ivanna Scare **HAUNTED HAPPENINGS**

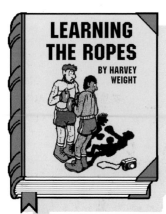

LEARNING THE ROPES

BY HARVEY WEIGHT

Sir Cumference KNIGHTS TO FORGET

A LONG HISTORY OF TIME

T. K. Tock

A History of Horticulture
by Dan DeLion

CHAPTER 2: DIVINATION

Some fortune-tellers predicted that the future was coming.

Dragons to WAGONS

The Story of Transportation

by Ellie Copter

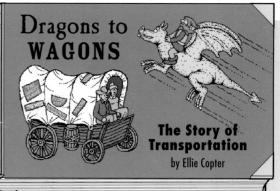

18 DIFFERENCES

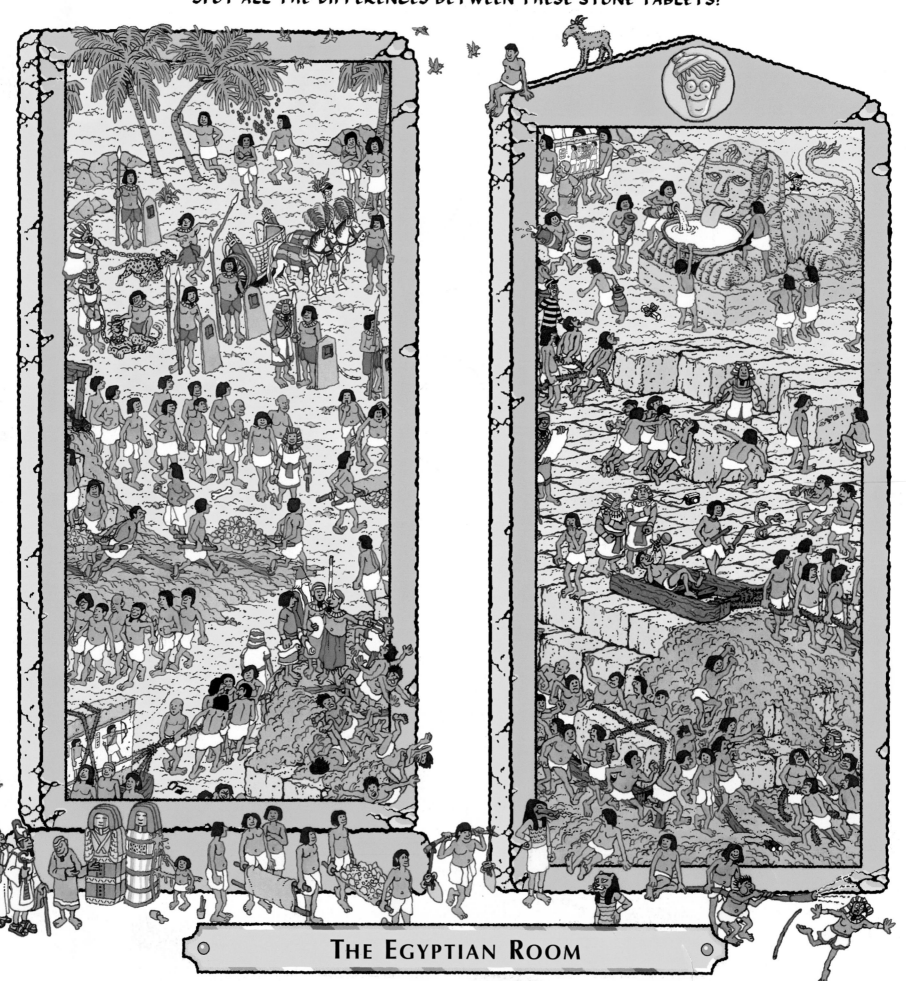

THE EGYPTIAN ROOM

Spot eight differences between each pair of tablets.

16 DIFFERENCES

FASHION SURE HAS CHANGED OVER THE YEARS,
BUT THESE FANCY FABRICS STILL LOOK FABULOUS!

COSTUMES AND CLOTHING

Spot the difference for each costume.

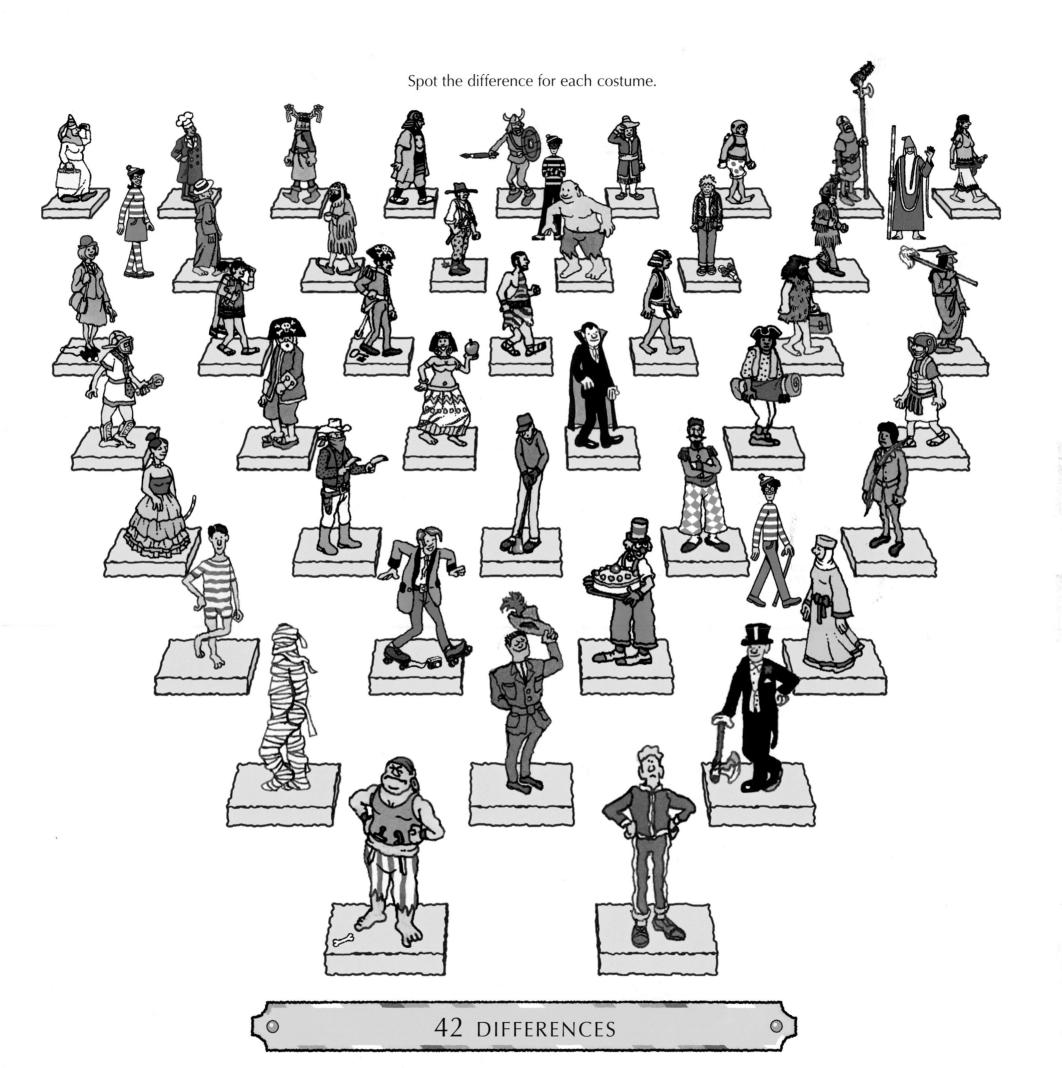

42 DIFFERENCES

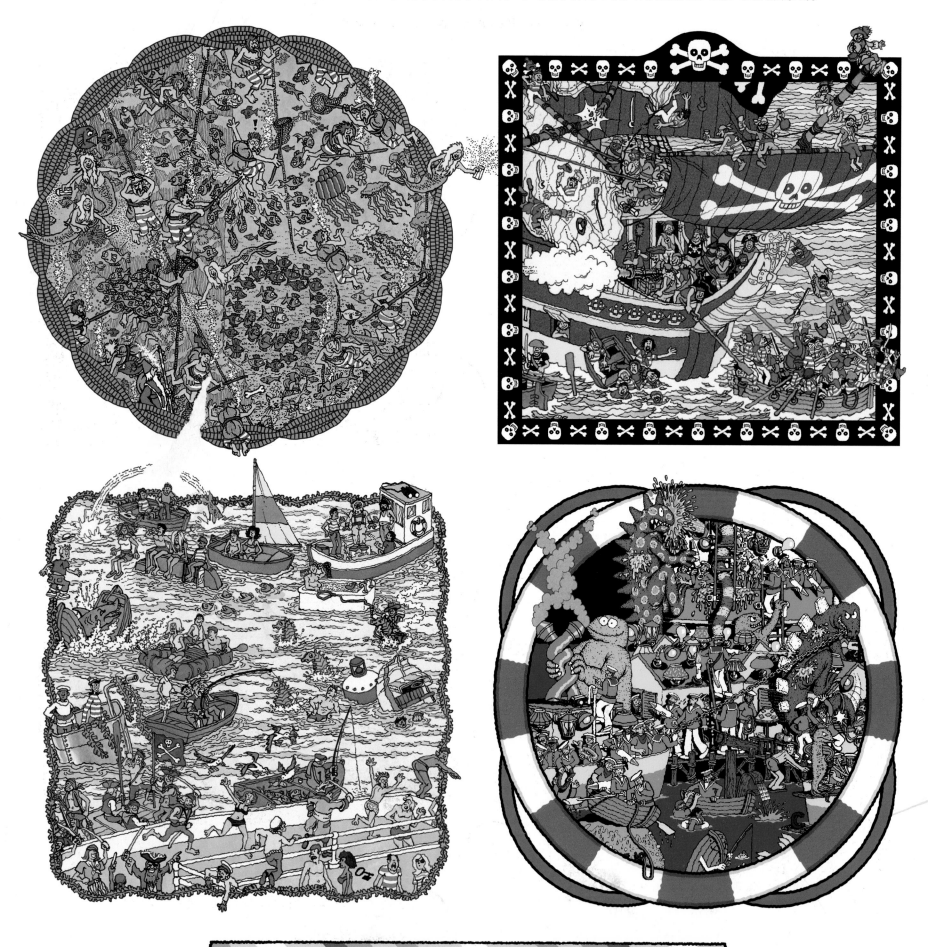

THE MARITIME COLLECTION

Spot five differences in each seascape.

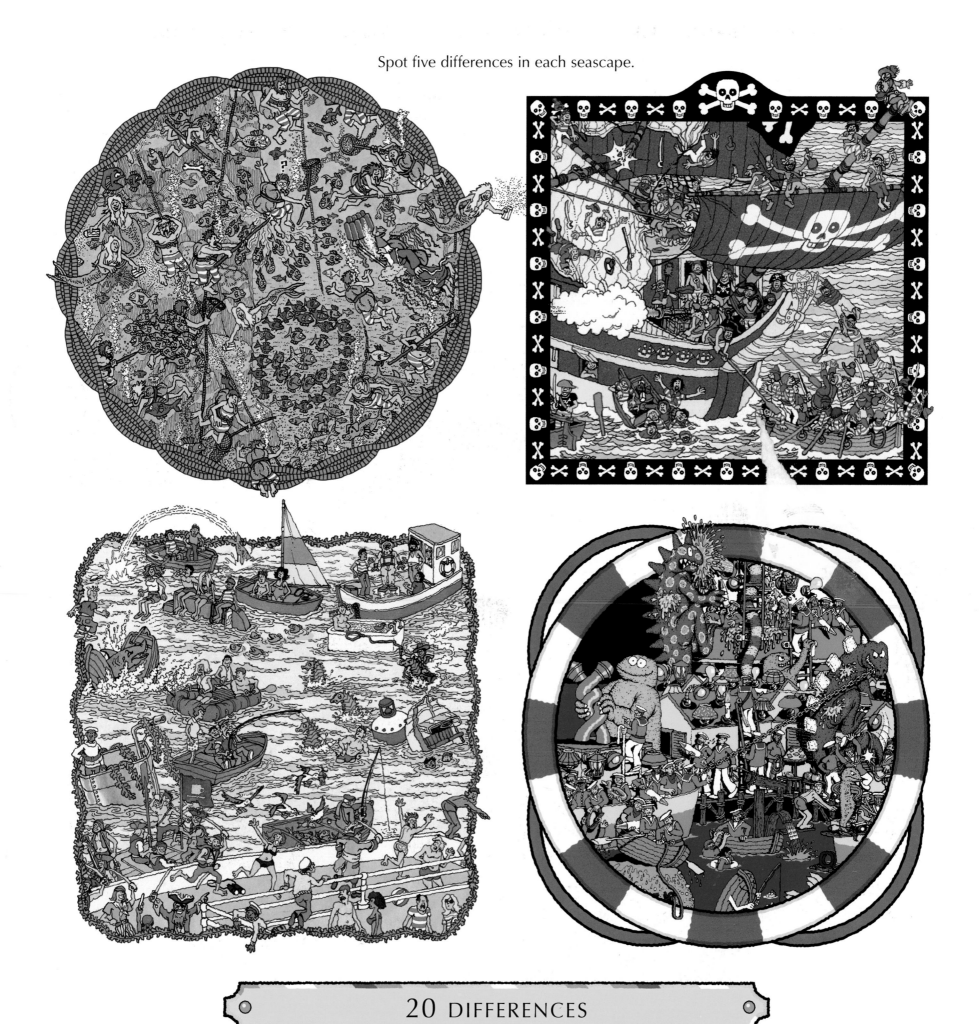

20 DIFFERENCES

SOMETHING'S A BIT OFF-KEY HERE. YOU'LL NEED TO CONDUCT A PROPER SEARCH TO FIND ALL THE DIFFERENCES. STAY SHARP!

Spot six differences among the pink army.

Spot six differences among the blue army.

MUSIC AND MELODY

Spot six differences among the drummers.

Spot two more differences . . . somewhere!

20 DIFFERENCES

ART THROUGH THE AGES AT ITS FINEST — THESE PAINTINGS HAVE REALLY COME ALIVE!

THE LONG GALLERY

Spot three differences for each painting.

30 DIFFERENCES

Spot six differences among the plants.

Spot six differences in the animals.

THE MUSEUM GARDENS

Spot six differences in the topiaries.

Spot six differences among the flower people.

Spot six more differences . . . somewhere!

30 DIFFERENCES

LAB COATS ON! WE'VE ENTERED THE SCIENCE ROOM!
THESE DIFFERENCES ARE A FORCE TO BE RECKONED WITH.

OUTER SPACE

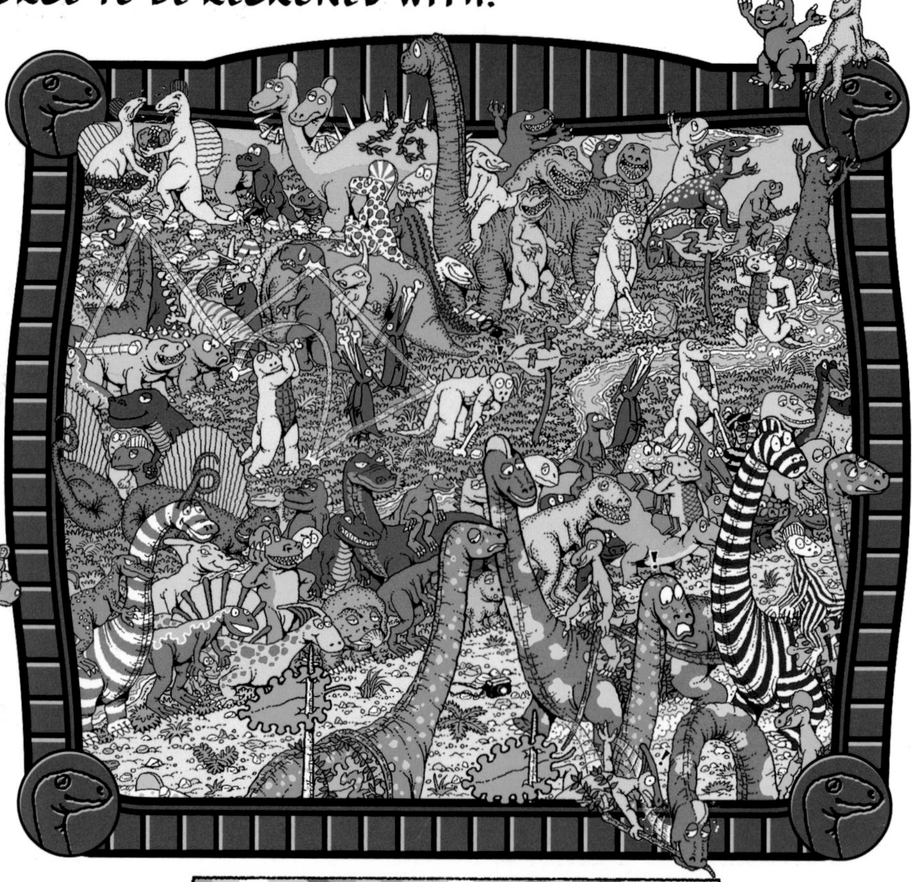

LATE JURASSIC

FORCES AND MOTION

CLONING

THE SCIENCE ROOM

Spot five differences in each exhibition.

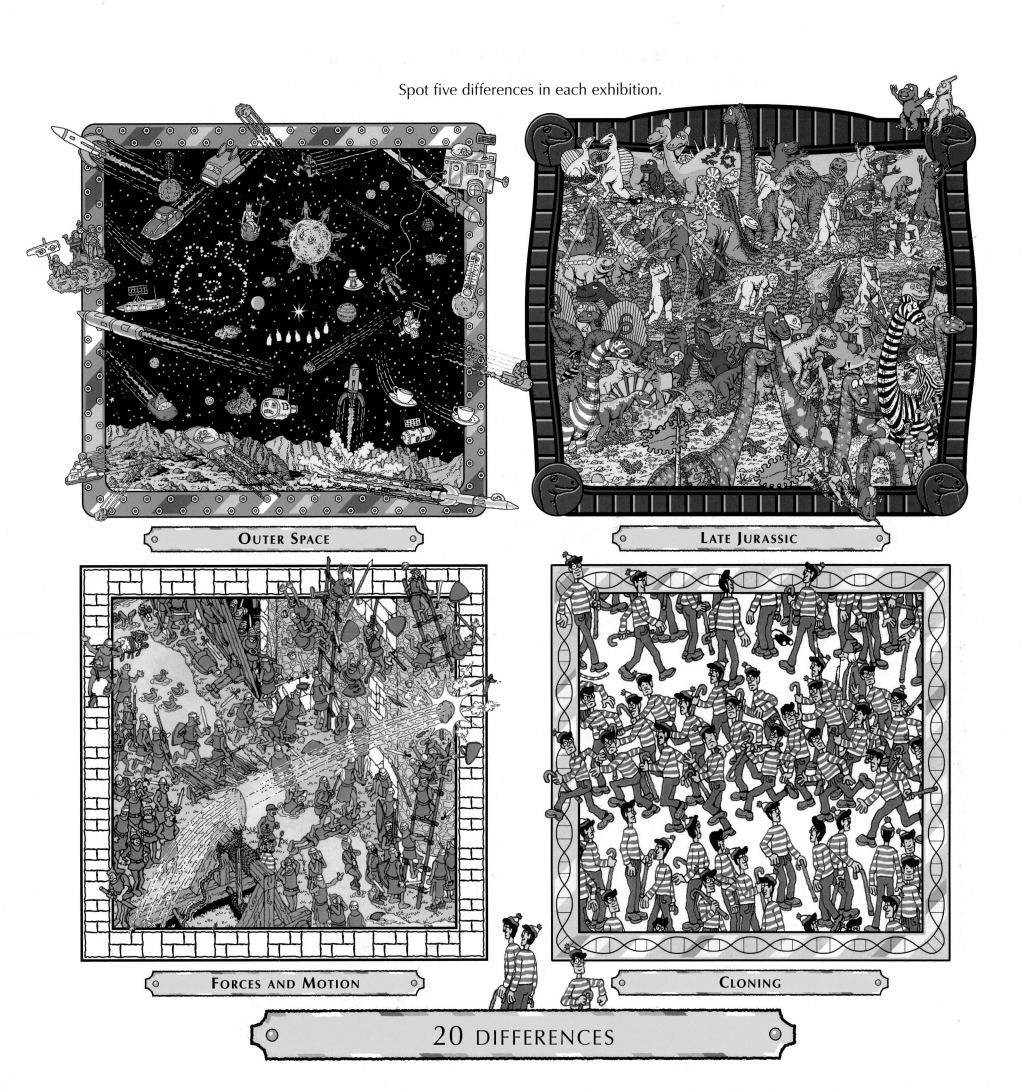

OUTER SPACE

LATE JURASSIC

FORCES AND MOTION

CLONING

20 DIFFERENCES

MY SKETCHES

SOME OF THE FLOWERS WEREN'T BLOOMING.

FORTUNATELY, THE GARDENERS GOT TO THE ROOT OF THE PROBLEM.

MAGNIFICENT AND MYSTERIOUS MONUMENTS!

FUN AT THE CASTLE...

WITH A GREAT KNIGHT LIFE!

WHAT A FANTASTIC FLAG!

FEARLESS AND FEROCIOUS VIKINGS, BARGE!

THIS EXHIBIT WAS DINO-MITE!

LOTS OF POTS!

MAGNIFICENT AND MYSTERIOUS MONUMENTS!

HERE ARE MY OWN SKETCHES FROM AROUND THE MUSEUM!

Spot two differences in each sketch.

26 DIFFERENCES

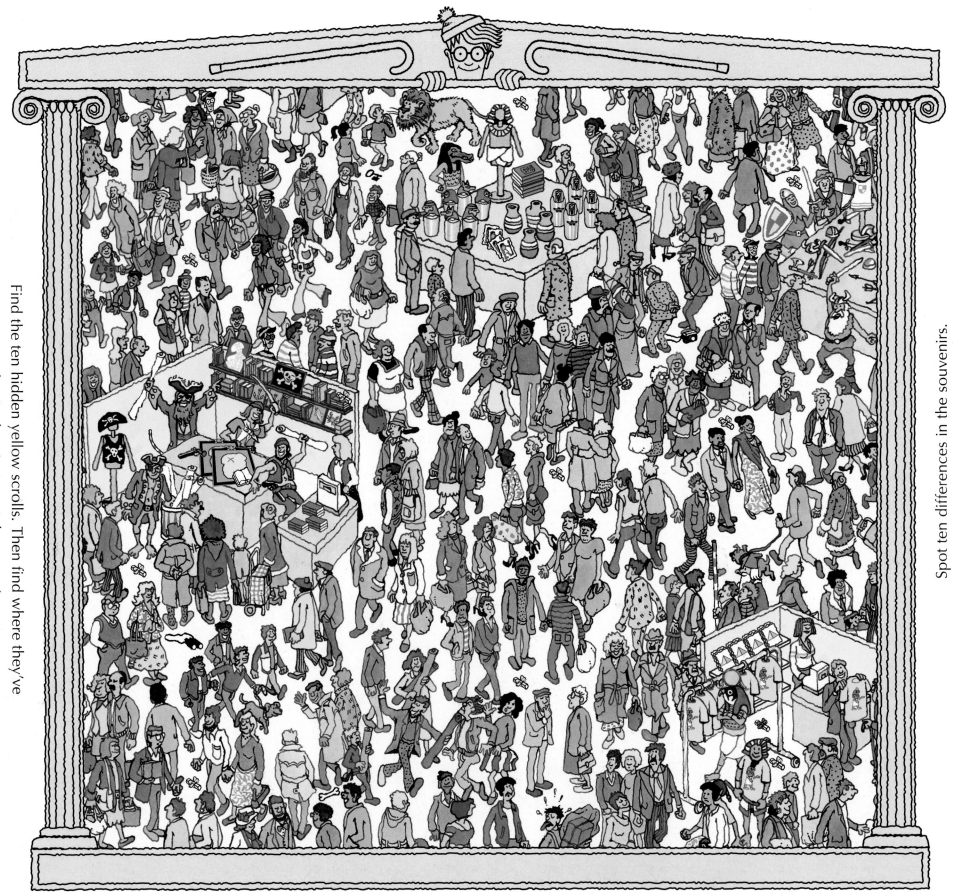

Find the ten hidden yellow scrolls. Then find where they've moved to in the picture on the opposite page.

Spot ten differences in the souvenirs.

THE GIFT SHOP

Spot ten differences in the shoppers.

Spot ten new characters on this side who have arrived from somewhere else in the museum. Then find which pages they came from!

50 DIFFERENCES

WHERE'S WALDO?

DOUBLE TROUBLE

AT THE MUSEUM

MARTIN HANDFORD

CHECKLISTS

Now that you've spotted all the differences, here are several more things to look for!

ONE LAST THING

Each picture on this spread has a match . . . except two things have changed! Can you spot the differences?

ONE FINAL, FINAL THING

Turn to the front cover and look at the painting above the museum balcony. Each painting has a slightly different double. Can you spot the differences between them?

THE ENTRANCE HALL

- [ ] A collapsing pillar
- [ ] A robbery in progress
- [ ] A dog on a leash
- [ ] Charioteers
- [ ] A drummer
- [ ] A toppling row of pots
- [ ] A poking painting
- [ ] Two shields
- [ ] Someone doing a handstand
- [ ] Someone in love with a person in a portrait

THE READING ROOM

- [ ] A ball gown
- [ ] A bag piper
- [ ] A horse-drawn carriage
- [ ] Shadow boxers
- [ ] A crocodile face
- [ ] Shrinking portions
- [ ] A waving dinosaur
- [ ] A red watering can
- [ ] A yellow watering can
- [ ] A bow tie

THE EGYPTIAN ROOM

- [ ] A thirsty sphinx
- [ ] Two horses
- [ ] A very loud horn
- [ ] Two sarcophagi
- [ ] A picture firing an arrow
- [ ] Dates falling from a tree
- [ ] Six workers pushing a block of stone
- [ ] Two snakes with their tongues out

COSTUMES AND CLOTHING

- [ ] One statue wearing green shoes
- [ ] Four statues wearing gloves
- [ ] Three statues with earrings
- [ ] Costumes with stripes
- [ ] Costumes with spots
- [ ] Costumes with buttons
- [ ] Costumes with belts
- [ ] Three skull-and-crossbones
- [ ] A blue bandana
- [ ] A red shield

THE MARITIME COLLECTION

- [ ] A golden sword
- [ ] A cat fish
- [ ] A dog fish
- [ ] Four seagulls
- [ ] A life preserver
- [ ] A cowboy riding a seahorse
- [ ] A fishing boat
- [ ] An inflatable duck
- [ ] A bathtub
- [ ] A sailor walking the plank

MUSIC AND MELODY

- [ ] Broken spears
- [ ] Spears held upside down
- [ ] A scythe
- [ ] A bowing accident
- [ ] A sharp accident
- [ ] Four soldiers who can't escape
- [ ] Two hats joined together
- [ ] Twenty-one horses
- [ ] People covering their ears
- [ ] A flying baton head
- [ ] A man wearing three hats

THE LONG GALLERY

- [ ] Two pears
- [ ] A blue handbag
- [ ] A ringing bell
- [ ] A broken drum
- [ ] A knight fighting a stag
- [ ] An ax in a door
- [ ] Characters in the wrong paintings
- [ ] Three people wearing yellow gloves

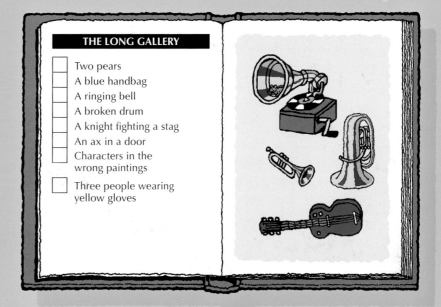

THE MUSEUM GARDENS

- [ ] Dandy lions
- [ ] A tree house
- [ ] A green house
- [ ] Flower beds
- [ ] A collision with a wheelbarrow
- [ ] People tripping on a hose
- [ ] A bull frog
- [ ] A spring onion
- [ ] A chicken laying an egg
- [ ] Someone tripping on flowerpots
- [ ] A hedgehog next to a hedge hog

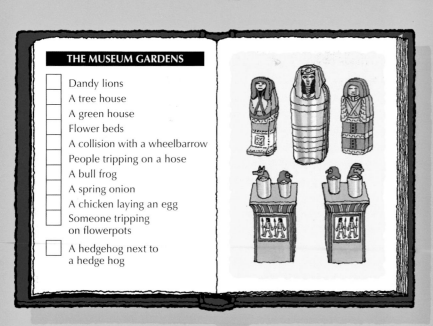

THE SCIENCE ROOM

- [ ] A game of golf
- [ ] Hitchhikers in the galaxy
- [ ] Three flattened soldiers
- [ ] A steeplechase race
- [ ] A battering ram
- [ ] Mercury
- [ ] Neptune
- [ ] A human bridge
- [ ] A traffic light
- [ ] A spacecraft on a collision course

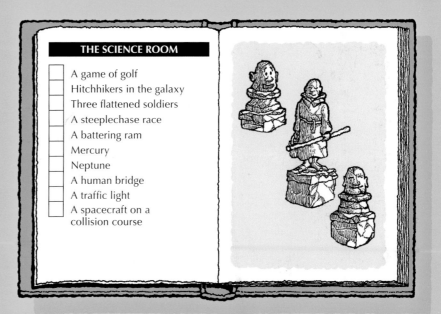

MY SKETCHES

- [ ] A flag within a flag
- [ ] A fish statue
- [ ] A skull-and-crossbones
- [ ] Drooping flowers
- [ ] Bows and arrows

THE GIFT SHOP

- [ ] A lion
- [ ] A dog with a striped collar
- [ ] A shopper with heavy packages
- [ ] A blue-and-yellow spotted bag
- [ ] A barefoot pirate
- [ ] Two yellow baskets

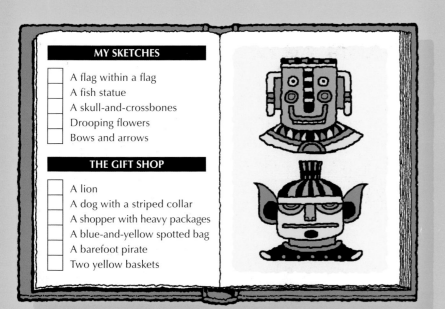

THE EXIT